For Rachel Claire
M.W.

*For Genevieve
and Asher*
B.F.

First published 1988 by
Walker Books Ltd
87 Vauxhall Walk
London SE11 5HJ

This edition published 1991

Printed in Hong Kong by Imago

British Library Cataloguing in Publication Data
Waddell, Martin
Can't you sleep, little bear?
I. Title   II. Firth, Barbara
823'.914 [J]   PZ7
ISBN 0-7445-1913-4

CAN'T YOU SLEEP, LITTLE BEAR?

Written by Martin Waddell
Illustrated by Barbara Firth

WALKER BOOKS
LONDON

Once there were two bears.
Big Bear and Little Bear.
Big Bear is the big bear, and Little Bear is the little bear.
They played all day in the bright sunlight. When night
came, and the sun went down, Big Bear took Little
Bear home to the Bear Cave.

Big Bear put Little Bear to bed
in the dark part of the cave.
"Go to sleep, Little Bear," he said.
And Little Bear tried.
Big Bear settled in the Bear Chair and
read his Bear Book, by the light of the fire.
But Little Bear couldn't get to sleep.

"Can't you sleep, Little Bear?"
asked Big Bear, putting down his Bear Book (which was just getting to the interesting part) and padding over to the bed.
"I'm scared," said Little Bear.
"Why are you scared, Little Bear?" asked Big Bear.
"I don't like the dark," said Little Bear.
"What dark?" said Big Bear.
"The dark all around us,"
said Little Bear.

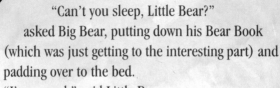

Big Bear looked, and he saw that the
dark part of the cave was very dark, so he went
to the Lantern Cupboard and took out the
tiniest lantern that was there.
Big Bear lit the tiniest lantern, and put it near
to Little Bear's bed.
"There's a tiny light to stop you being scared,
Little Bear," said Big Bear.
"Thank you, Big Bear," said Little Bear,
cuddling up in the glow.
"Now go to sleep, Little Bear," said Big Bear,
and he padded back to the Bear Chair and
settled down to read the Bear Book,
by the light of the fire.

Little Bear tried to
go to sleep, but he couldn't.

"Can't you sleep, Little Bear?" yawned Big Bear,
putting down his Bear Book (with just four pages to
go to the interesting bit) and padding over to the bed.

"I'm scared," said Little Bear.

"Why are you scared, Little Bear?" asked Big Bear.

"I don't like the dark," said Little Bear.

"What dark?" said Big Bear.

"The dark all around us," said Little Bear.

"But I brought you a lantern!" said Big Bear.

"Only a tiny-weeny one," said Little Bear. "And
there's lots of dark!"

Big Bear looked, and he saw that Little Bear was
quite right, there was still lots of dark. So Big Bear
went to the Lantern Cupboard and took out
a bigger lantern. Big Bear lit the lantern, and
put it beside the other one.

"Now go to sleep, Little Bear," said Big Bear
and he padded back to the Bear Chair and settled
down to read the Bear Book, by the light of the fire.
Little Bear tried and tried to go to sleep,
but he couldn't.

"Can't you sleep, Little Bear?" grunted Big Bear, putting down his Bear Book (with just three pages to go) and padding over to the bed.

"I'm scared," said Little Bear.

"Why are you scared, Little Bear?" asked Big Bear.

"I don't like the dark," said Little Bear.

"What dark?" asked Big Bear.

"The dark all around us," said Little Bear.

"But I brought you two lanterns!" said Big Bear. "A tiny one and a bigger one!"

"Not much bigger," said Little Bear. "And there's still lots of dark."

Big Bear thought about it, and then
he went to the Lantern Cupboard
and took out the Biggest Lantern of
Them All, with two handles and a
bit of chain. He hooked the
lantern up above Little Bear's bed.
"I've brought you the Biggest Lantern
of Them All!" he told Little Bear.
"That's to stop you being scared!"
"Thank you, Big Bear," said Little
Bear, curling up in the glow and
watching the shadows dance.
"Now go to sleep, Little Bear," said Big
Bear and he padded back to the Bear
Chair and settled down to read the
Bear Book, by the light
of the fire.

Little Bear tried and tried and
tried to go to sleep,
but he couldn't.

"Can't you sleep, Little Bear?" groaned Big Bear,
putting down his Bear Book
(with just two pages to go)
   and padding over to the bed.

"I'm scared," said Little Bear.
"Why are you scared, Little Bear?" asked Big Bear.
"I don't like the dark," said Little Bear.
"What dark?" asked Big Bear.
"The dark all around us," said Little Bear.
"But I brought you the Biggest Lantern of Them All,
and there isn't any dark left," said Big Bear.
"Yes, there is!" said Little Bear. "There is, out there!"
And he pointed out of the Bear Cave, at the night.

Big Bear saw that Little Bear was right.

Big Bear was very puzzled. All the lanterns in
the world couldn't light up the dark outside.
Big Bear thought about it for a long time, and
then he said, "Come on, Little Bear."

"Where are we going?" asked Little Bear.

"Out!" said Big Bear.

"Out into the darkness?" said Little Bear.

"Yes!" said Big Bear.

"But I'm scared of the dark!" said Little Bear.

"No need to be!" said Big Bear, and he took
Little Bear by the paw and led him out from
the cave into the night

and it was...

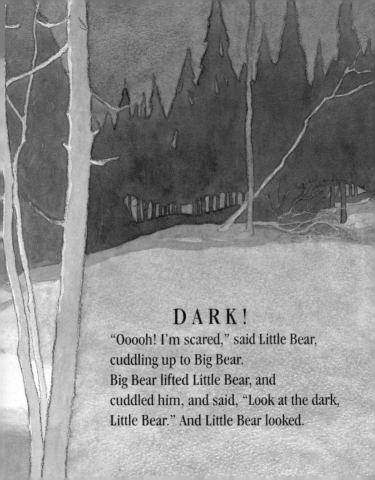

DARK!

"Ooooh! I'm scared," said Little Bear,
cuddling up to Big Bear.
Big Bear lifted Little Bear, and
cuddled him, and said, "Look at the dark,
Little Bear." And Little Bear looked.

"I've brought you the moon, Little Bear," said Big Bear.
"The bright yellow moon, and all the twinkly stars."

But Little Bear didn't say anything, for he had gone
to sleep, warm and safe in Big Bear's arms.
Big Bear carried Little Bear back into the Bear Cave,
fast asleep, and he settled down with Little Bear
on one arm and the Bear Book on the other, cosy
in the Bear Chair by the fire.

And Big Bear read the Bear Book right to...

THE END